Hockey's H[ot] Goalies

by James Duplacey

Tom Barrasso

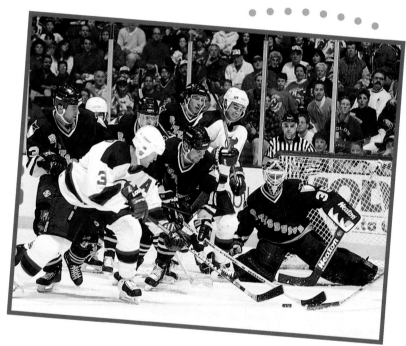

Most goalies spend time in other pro leagues before making it to the NHL. Not Tom Barrasso. He went straight to the NHL from high school. Experts said Barrasso could not handle the pressure. He proved them wrong. Barrasso won the rookie-of-the-year and top goalie awards.

During the 1996–97 season, Barrasso injured his shoulder. He tried to keep playing, but he was not very good. People thought his career was over. Again, Barrasso did what he had to do. He proved them wrong.

Barrasso had surgery to fix his shoulder. At first, he could not raise his arm over his head. But slowly Barrasso began to get healthy.

Barrasso is tall and has a long reach.

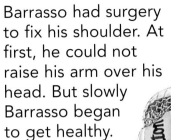

By the 1997–98 season, the old Barrasso was back. He could snap out his glove hand without feeling pain. Barrasso allowed an average of only two goals per game. He stopped more than 92 percent of all the shots he faced.

Barrasso is a top goalie again. He plays best when the pressure is on. Barrasso's teammates know they can count on him. He will not prove them wrong.

Ed Belfour

Ed Belfour's nickname is "the Eagle." It suits him. Watch him swoop across his net to make a save. Belfour protects his crease the way an eagle protects its nest.

This top netminder is known as a stand-up goalie. That means Belfour does not dive or flop around in his crease. Instead, he stands solidly with his knees tucked in, forming a V shape. Belfour is a strong, fast skater. That speed helps him move quickly from post to post.

Belfour has won the Vezina Trophy for top goalie twice.

Belfour keeps his glove hand low. This leaves the top part of the net open. The Eagle knows that his quick glove can snare most high shots.

No other goalie uses his stick the way Belfour does. Watch him when opposing forwards are swarming the net. Belfour will crouch down and place his stick along the ice. Then he will use it to block and clear loose pucks.

After injuries slowed him down, Belfour began to train harder. His work paid off. During the 1997–98 season, he had a career-high nine shutouts and allowed an average of fewer than two goals per game. What a star!

Martin Brodeur

This smooth goaltender never seems to waste a move. Martin Brodeur does not dive across his net. He just nudges his pad out or sneaks a glove up. Brodeur tucks in his knees and keeps the puck out. He makes goaltending look easy.

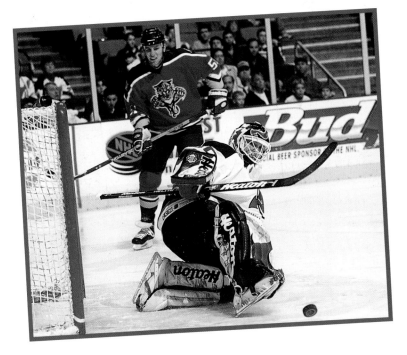

Brodeur's dad was a practice netminder with the Montreal Canadiens. He saw great goalies such as Jacques Plante play. He taught his son to play that same classic stand-up style. Thanks to this training, Brodeur stays solid on his skates and challenges shooters.

Of course, Brodeur has created his own style, too. He uses the butterfly to cover the lower part of the net. This means that he stands low to the ice with his pads spread in a V shape.

Cool and calm — that is also Brodeur's style. He is not a flashy goalkeeper. But in the 1997–98 season, he won 43 games. Only two other goalies have won more games in a season.

Brodeur has had back-to-back seasons with at least ten shutouts. Those results could earn him a place in the Hockey Hall of Fame.

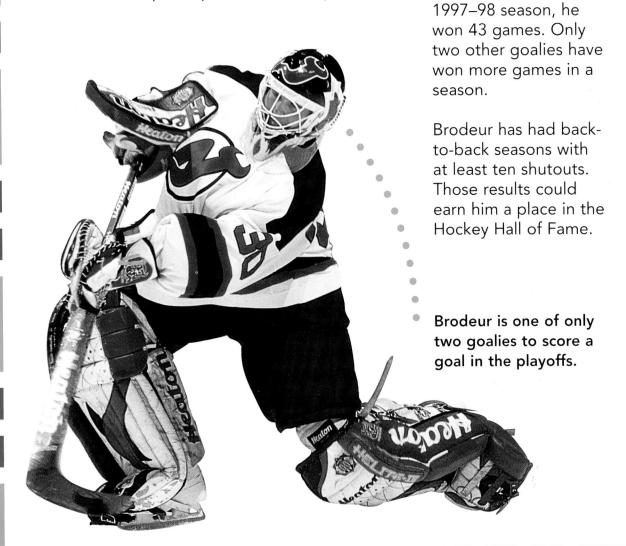

Brodeur is one of only two goalies to score a goal in the playoffs.

Byron Dafoe

It took a long time for Byron Dafoe to become a top NHL goalie. Early in his career, he did not see much ice time. That was tough, because young goalies need to play a lot. If they don't, they can lose their confidence. That is exactly what happened to Dafoe.

Then Dafoe was traded to Boston. He was told he could play even if he gave up bad goals. That helped Dafoe relax. Now he is one of the NHL's best young netminders.

"Lord Byron" has a stand-up style. Some other goalies challenge the shooter. Some flop around in the net. Dafoe waits until the opposing player makes his move. Then he makes his.

Dafoe can dare to wait because he has great reflexes. With his quick feet, he can speedily slide from post to post. With his lightning-fast glove hand, Dafoe can easily snare any high shots.

In Dafoe's first year in Boston, he played in 65 games. Few goalies play that many. Dafoe had six shutouts. That is the most shutouts by a Boston goalie in 16 years.

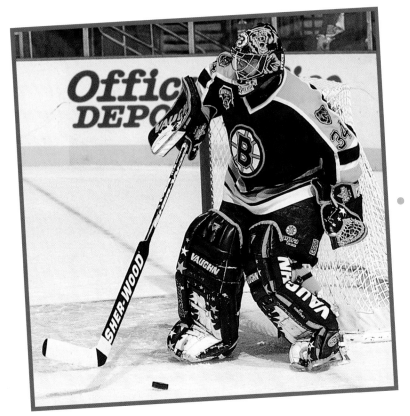

Dafoe is one of the few NHL players born in England.

Grant Fuhr

Most goalies slow down as they get older. Not Grant Fuhr. He is playing better than he did five years ago. In the 1996–97 season, Fuhr played 79 games. That is more than any goalie in the NHL's history.

Fuhr can get to his feet quickly after he drops to make a save.

One reason Fuhr is at the top of his game is his tough fitness program. Fuhr has a personal trainer to keep him in top shape. Staying fit allows him to play so many games. It makes Fuhr flexible, too.

Fuhr is also a great netminder because he is smart. He studies the other teams. When enemy forwards race toward Fuhr's net, he is ready. He faces the shooter straight on. Fuhr leaves forwards no room to tuck in the puck.

Unlike almost all NHL goalies, Fuhr catches with his right hand. This confuses opposing forwards. They expect a goalie's right to be his weak side. Not when they face Fuhr.

Even when his team's defense lets shooters through, Fuhr comes up with big saves. This talent has earned Fuhr the Vezina Trophy for top goaltender.

Dominik Hasek

There has never been a goalie like Dominik Hasek. He dives and twists around his goal crease like a human pretzel.

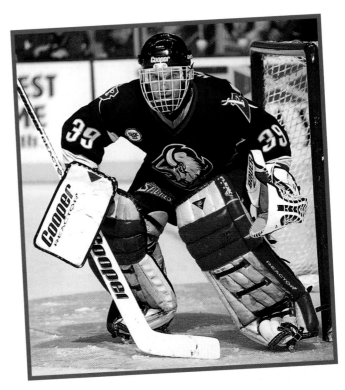

Even when Hasek is sprawled on the ice, he is in control. He anchors a skate inside each post. No shot can sneak through. He will even drop his stick along the goal line to stop pucks from rolling in.

Hasek's great reflexes make it tough for shooters to put the puck past him.

Shooters cannot predict Hasek's next move. That makes it tough for them to put a puck past him. As well, Hasek will stop the puck with any part of his body. He even uses his mask!

Most goalies use their catching gloves to freeze loose pucks. Not "the Dominator." Hasek uses the blocker because it has a glove with fingers. That way, he can feel the puck. This lets Hasek know that he has the puck completely covered.

The 1997–98 season was Hasek's greatest. This Czech netminder led his country to the gold medal in the 1998 Winter Olympics. He won his second straight Hart Trophy as the NHL's top player. And the Dominator won his fourth Vezina Trophy as the NHL's top goalie.

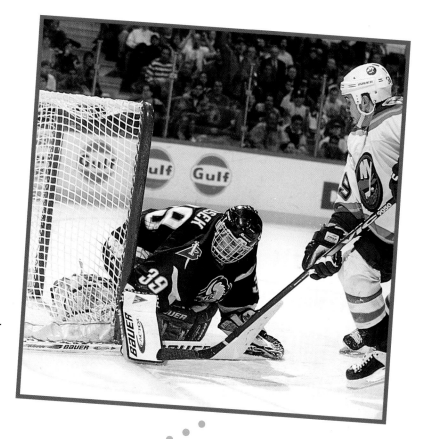

Curtis Joseph

Fans love to watch Curtis Joseph play goal. He will do anything to keep the puck out of the net. "Cujo" will dive across the crease to stop a shot. He will slide far out of the net to snare a loose puck. Joseph will even take a puck on the mask if it keeps the puck out of the net.

Joseph is not showing off or "hotdogging" with these amazing moves. He just wants to stop the puck. It does not matter to Joseph how he does it.

Joseph has quick feet and fast hands.

Experts call Joseph a reaction goalie. He lets the play come to him. Then Cujo decides how to play the shot. With his great reflexes and ability, Joseph can adjust to any situation.

Cujo catches left-handed, but he shoots right-handed. That means he must change hands on his stick when he shoots the puck. Joseph holds the top of the stick with his catching glove and the bottom with his blocker. The puck really moves when he fires it this way.

With his great smile and wide-open style, Joseph will be a fan favorite for a very long time.

Nikolai Khabibulin

Nikolai Khabibulin never played baseball as a kid. But he plays goal as if he did. Like a good infielder, Khabibulin crouches low, slowly shuffling his feet. Like a top shortstop, he does not lie back.

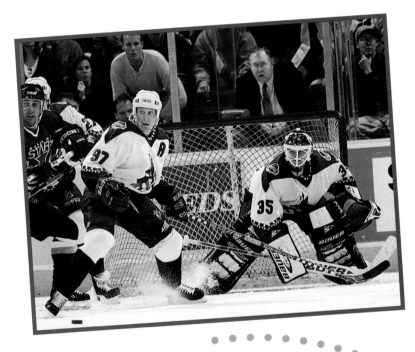

Khabibulin moves out of his crease and attacks shooters. By doing this, he catches opposing forwards off guard. Shooters usually end up firing the puck right into "Khabie's" pads. That is just what he wants them to do.

Among his teammates, Khabibulin is known as "the Bulin Wall." He blocks just about everything that is fired his way. With his long arms and legs, Russian-born Khabie can cover a lot of net. Even if he is caught out of position, he can reach almost any shot.

In the 1996–97 season, Khabie set a Phoenix club record with seven shutouts.

If the Bulin Wall had his way, he would play every game. He almost did during the 1997–98 season. Khabie played in 70 games for the Phoenix Coyotes. This is the second-highest number of games played in a season by a goalie born outside North America.

With his love of the game, Khabibulin should be donning the pads for many more years.

Trevor Kidd

It takes more than talent to make it as a goalie in the NHL. Trevor Kidd knows that. He has a lot of talent. But when he hit the big league, he had no success. Kidd had played well in junior hockey and with Team Canada. When he went to the NHL, he lost his confidence.

Then Kidd lost his job with the Calgary Flames. The team traded him to the Carolina Hurricanes. Kidd was pleased to be traded. Finally, he was with a team that wanted him. Kidd's confidence soared.

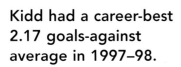

Kidd had a career-best 2.17 goals-against average in 1997–98.

During the 1997–98 season, Kidd was on top of his game. In the past, he would lunge at shooters. He has learned to stand his ground. Kidd forces forwards to make mistakes.

Patience is another thing that Kidd has learned. Before, he used to fire the puck around the glass. Kidd has taught himself to take his time. He makes sure that every play is the right play.

Best of all, Kidd has let his natural talent take over. This talent will keep him at the top for a long time.

Olaf Kolzig

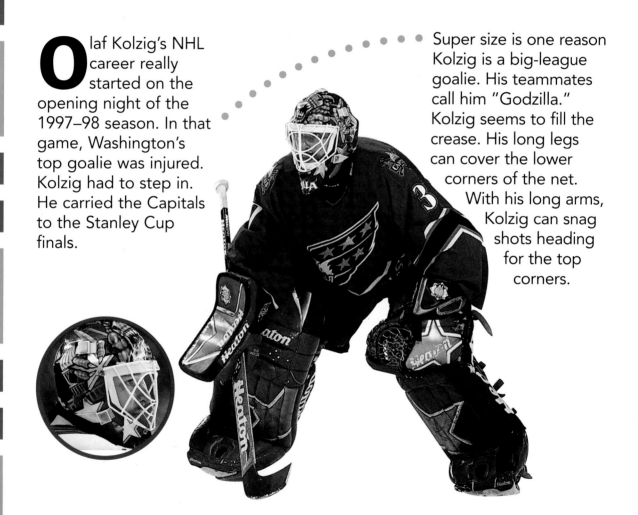

Olaf Kolzig's NHL career really started on the opening night of the 1997–98 season. In that game, Washington's top goalie was injured. Kolzig had to step in. He carried the Capitals to the Stanley Cup finals.

Super size is one reason Kolzig is a big-league goalie. His teammates call him "Godzilla." Kolzig seems to fill the crease. His long legs can cover the lower corners of the net. With his long arms, Kolzig can snag shots heading for the top corners.

Kolzig leaves just a little space between his legs. He almost dares shooters to go for it. When they do, Godzilla drops into the butterfly position, with his legs in a V shape. No goal.

Before the 1997–98 season, Kolzig had never had much steady playing time. He made the most of his chance that season. Kolzig appeared in 64 games. He allowed an average of just over two goals per game.

Kolzig is quick and smooth on his skates.

It was in the playoffs that Kolzig made his name. He won 12 games and had 4 shutouts. Those are team records for the Caps. Washington has a monster talent in Godzilla.

Chris Osgood

In 1997, the Detroit Red Wings won the Stanley Cup with Mike Vernon in net. The next season, Chris Osgood took over. He had to fill Vernon's skates. It was not easy, and it was not fun.

People were watching Osgood's every move. He just kept playing. "Ozzie" has great confidence in his skills. That helps him beat the pressure.

In 1996, Osgood scored an empty-net goal against Hartford.

In the 1998 playoffs, Osgood let in a couple of easy goals from center ice. The fans booed and yelled at Ozzie. But he never let it get to him. That is a skill no one can teach. In fact, Osgood is known for coming through in the crunch.

Much of Ozzie's success comes from his solid style. He is also speedy. Ozzie's lightning-fast glove hand lets him snare hot shots. His quick feet allow him to adjust to any shot.

The key to Osgood's success is his will to win. This desire helped him lead the Red Wings back into the Stanley Cup winner's circle in 1998. It will keep Osgood in the NHL for many more seasons.

Damian Rhodes

Did you know that Damian Rhodes refuses to look at the time clock during a game? Or that he spends the night before an important home game in a hotel? These are not superstitions to "Dusty" Rhodes. They are things he feels he must do to prepare for a game.

Focus and routine are key to the way Rhodes plays.

On the ice, Rhodes rarely moves between breaks in the action. He does not pace back and forth in the crease, the way most goalies do. Instead, Rhodes saves his energy. This helps him make tough saves, even late in a game.

Rhodes is known as a stand-up goalie. He stands solidly in the net and rarely sprawls on the ice. This style means that Dusty has to be in position and ready for every shot.

Before each game, Rhodes studies the players on the other team. He learns where they shoot. He memorizes how they like to pass. When Dusty hits the ice, he knows what he must do to stop every player.

The 1997–98 season was Dusty's finest in the NHL. He helped the Ottawa Senators win their first playoff series. Rhodes also set a team record with five shutouts.

Mike Richter

In the summer of 1998, Mike Richter was a free agent, and many teams wanted to sign him. He decided to stay in New York. Ranger fans are glad he did.

In 1994, Richter led the Rangers to a Stanley Cup win. Fans hope he will guide the team to another top trophy soon.

Two reasons Richter is so good are his legs. They look like tree trunks. They allow Richter to move with great speed from side to side. He knows he has to protect those legs. Richter has had some tough muscle pulls in his career. So he works extra hard to stay in top shape.

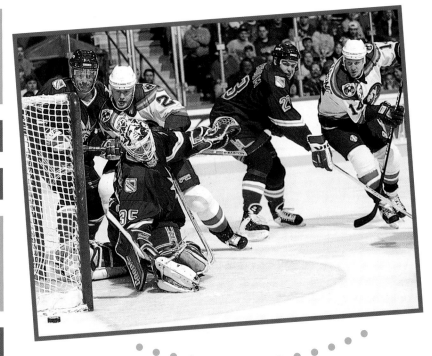

Few goalies protect the corners better than Richter.

Richter also uses his blocker more than most goalies. Because he sometimes gives up big rebounds, Richter tries to deflect the puck into the corner. That allows his defensemen to reach the puck before the other team does.

Richter is not big, but he can cover the whole net. He does the splits better than any other goalie. He goes much lower than other netminders. He also gets back on his feet more quickly.

Patrick Roy

It has been a long time since Patrick Roy began his NHL career back in 1985. Not much has changed. Roy still twists his neck like a bird. He still talks to his goalposts for good luck. He still wins.

Roy has a unique style. To stop pucks, he drops to his knees and stretches his pads from post to post. That position lets him stop low shots. Roy uses his upper body, blocker and glove to stop the high shots. This style has made "Saint Patrick" a top goalie.

One of the fastest glove hands in all of hockey belongs to Roy. With that speedy mitt, he can snare shots from any angle.

What else does it take to be a winning goalie like Roy? He has lots of confidence. Roy believes that no one can put the puck past him, even in overtime. Having legs like steel springs also helps Roy be a winner.

All of these things make Roy a top goalie. He has won more playoff games than any other goaltender. Roy's talent has also put his name on the Stanley Cup three times.

Roy has won the Vezina Trophy for top NHL goalie three times.

John Vanbiesbrouck

John Vanbiesbrouck is one of the shortest goaltenders in the NHL. He stands just 1.7 m (5 ft. 8 in.) tall. "The Beezer" may be short, but he has huge skills.

Because he does not have great size, Vanbiesbrouck relies on technique. His positioning and reflexes must be top-notch. The Beezer is very aggressive. He challenges shooters, forcing them to make the first move.

Few goalies have better reflexes than Vanbiesbrouck. Even if he is caught out of position, he is able to react swiftly. Quick as a flash, he will get set for a shot.

The Beezer is also a magician with his stick. In his hands, it is like a magic wand. That wand can clip enemy ankles. It can also poke away loose pucks and break up passes.

Few goalies play with more heart and will to win than Vanbiesbrouck. After a poor 1997–98 season, he refused to make excuses. The Beezer just said, "I will be better next year." The Philadelphia Flyers like his confidence. That is why they signed Vanbiesbrouck as their top goalie.

The Beezer studies shooters and learns their shooting patterns.

To Lionel Romain — JD

Text copyright © 1999 by Dan Diamond and Associates, Inc.

We acknowledge the support of the Canada Council for the Arts and the Ontario Arts Council for our publishing program.

Published in Canada by
Kids Can Press Ltd.
29 Birch Avenue
Toronto, ON M4V 1E2

Published in the U.S. by
Kids Can Press Ltd.
85 River Rock Drive, Suite 202
Buffalo, NY 14207

All photos courtesy of Bruce Bennett Studios, except pages 14 and 15 courtesy of Dave Sandford/Hockey Hall of Fame

Edited by Elizabeth MacLeod
Designed by Julia Naimska

Printed in Hong Kong by Sheck Wah Tong Printing Press Limited.

CM PA 99 0 9 8 7 6 5 4 3 2 1

Canadian Cataloguing in Publication Data

Duplacey, James
        Goalies

(Hockey's hottest)
Includes foldout banner of Hockey's hottest goalies.
ISBN 1-55074-561-1

1. Hockey goalkeepers – Biography – Juvenile literature. 2. National Hockey League – Juvenile literature. I. Title. II. Series: Duplacey, James. Hockey's hottest.

GV848.5.A1D88   1999e   j796.962'092'2   C99-930156-X

Kids Can Press is a Nelvana company